THE GIR[...] TO THE UNDERWORLD

THE GIRL WHO LOVED FOOD

RETOLD BY POMME CLAYTON

ILLUSTRATED BY TONY ROSS

ORCHARD BOOKS

For my cousin Rosie
P.C.

Orchard Books
96 Leonard Street, London EC2A 4XD
Orchard Books Australia
14 Mars Road, Lane Cove, NSW 2066
The text was first published in Great Britain in the form of a
gift collection called Tales of Amazing Maidens,
illustrated by Sophie Herxheimer in 1995.
This edition published in 1999
1 86039 682 8 (hardback)
1 86039 862 6 (paperback)
Text © Pomme Clayton 1995
Illustrations © Tony Ross 1998
The rights of Pomme Clayton to be identified as the author
and Tony Ross to be identified as the illustrator have been
asserted by them in accordance with the
Copyright, Designs and Patents Act, 1988.
A CIP catalogue record for this book is available from the British Library
1 3 5 7 9 10 8 6 4 2 (hardback)
1 3 5 7 9 10 8 6 4 2 (paperback)
Printed in Great Britain

THE GIRL WHO WENT TO THE UNDERWORLD

Anansi is half man, half spider, but one hundred per cent greedy. He can change his shape whenever he wants, but he is always getting into trouble.

One summer it was very hot. The sun burnt like a giant furnace. There wasn't a cloud in the sky and it hadn't rained for months. The streams dried up, the crops withered and there was nothing left to eat. Nothing in Mrs Anansi's cupboards, nothing in the garden, and nothing in the fields. So Anansi sent his children to look for food.

Anansi's eldest daughter went into the forest. It was cool and shady. She looked on bushes for fruit and under stones for roots. But she didn't find anything. Then she saw a nut tree. But when she got closer, the tree only had three nuts. "Three nuts will not feed my family," she sighed. "but if I eat the nuts myself, at least I will have more strength to look for food."

So Anansi's Daughter picked the nuts, and found a stone to crack the shells. She crouched on the ground and brought the stone down – *crack* – on the first nut. It bounced down a large hole. "Oh, bother!" she said.

She brought the stone down – *crack* – on the second nut, and that bounced down the hole. "Oh bother!" she cried. "If this last nut jumps down that hole, I'll jump down there myself and get it back!" And – *crack* – the third nut flew down the hole!

At that, Anansi's
Daughter peered
into the hole. It
was so dark she
couldn't see the
bottom. But she
took a deep breath
and jumped. It was
a long way down.
A very long way
down. She fell
through a starry
sky, she fell past
the moon, past
leaves and through
branches. She
tumbled into a
sunny day, and
landed on a soft
mossy bank.

Anansi's Daughter had fallen into the underworld.

She rubbed her eyes and saw a lush green field and a little hut. Beside the hut sat a wrinkled old woman cracking nuts with her teeth.

"Mmmm hmmm, delicious!" said the old woman.

Anansi's Daughter thought that the nuts looked just like the ones she'd lost. But she said nothing.

"Are you hungry?" asked the old woman. Anansi's Daughter nodded.

"Well, there are lots of sweet potatoes growing in the field," the old woman replied. "The big potatoes will be calling '*Eat me*!' and the little potatoes will be calling '*Don't eat me!*' Take this spade, dig up the little potatoes and bring them to me."

Anansi's Daughter took the spade, and went into the field. She saw huge, juicy potatoes calling out "*Eat me, eat me!*" She was starving and they looked tasty.

Then she saw tiny, shrivelled potatoes calling out *"Don't eat me, don't eat me!"* They did not look tasty at all. But she remembered what the old woman had said, and dug the little potatoes up.

"Now, child," said the old woman. "Peel the potatoes. Put the peel in the pot, and throw away the insides."

Anansi's Daughter had never heard of a recipe like that before. But she peeled the potatoes, threw away the wizened insides, and put the muddy peel into the pot. The pot began to bubble. Then Anansi's Daughter poured the peelings into two bowls, and they sat down to eat.

The old woman picked up her spoon and ate, but not with her mouth. She began eating through her nose, and eating through her ears! Anansi's Daughter had never seen eating like that before. But she was very polite, and said nothing. She picked up her spoon, and wondered what muddy potato peelings would taste like.

"Mmmm hmmm, delicious!" she cried.

They were the tastiest thing she had ever eaten.

"Thank you, child," said the old woman. "I would like to give you something in return." She showed Anansi's Daughter a door at the back of the hut "Go inside, and choose the smallest drum."

Anansi's Daughter opened the door. Inside was a room full of drums. Drums of every size and shape. Huge drums decorated with carvings, medium-sized drums with curved sticks and coloured skins, and little drums covered in beads and tinkling bells. Then she saw the smallest drum. It was old, and worn, and plain. Anansi's Daughter badly wanted one of the big, beautiful drums, but she remembered what the old woman had said, and chose the smallest plainest drum.

"Take the drum home, play it, and shout *COVER!*" advised the old woman.

Then she showed Anansi's Daughter a
path that led into the forest. Anansi's
Daughter thanked the old woman, and set
off with the little drum under her arm.

She had hardly taken a few steps along
the path, when she found herself back in
our world. There were her father, Anansi,
her mother and brothers and sisters.

"What have you got?" they cried.

She showed them her drum.

"A drum!" sneered Anansi. "What
good is that? We're hungry, we want food,
not music."

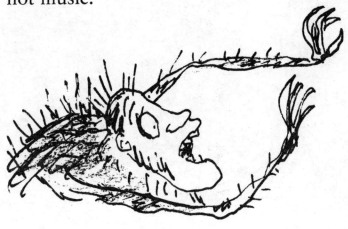

But Anansi's Daughter sat on the
ground and began to play the drum.
Ta te, ta te te, ta ta taa.
Faster and faster and faster.
Ta te, ta te te, ta ta TAA!
"Cover!" she cried.

Suddenly the whole floor was covered
with food. There was rice and peas, dried
saltfish and dumplings, spicy patties and
plantain, fresh pineapple and cool
sarsaparilla juice to wash it all down.
Everyone was amazed. But not for long!

They fell on the food and feasted until there wasn't a crumb left. Then they all lay down to doze in the sun.

Everyone except Anansi. Because Anansi was thinking to himself, "Where did she get such a wonderful drum?"

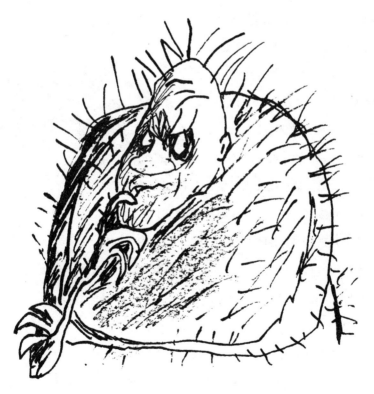

The next day Anansi's Daughter told her father the whole story. All about the nuts, and the hole and... But before she had time to finish, Anansi had run off into the forest.

He found the tree, and sure enough, there were only three nuts on it. He picked them, took a stone and brought it down – *crack* – on the first nut. It did not jump down the hole. The shell cracked, and out popped a juicy nut. Anansi ate it.

"Mmmm hmmm, delicious!"

He brought the stone down – *crack* – on the second nut, and ate that. Then – *crack* – and the third nut was in his mouth. He picked up all the shells and threw them down the hole, then peered into the darkness. "I am not jumping down there," he grumbled.

So he turned himself into a spider and spun a web, then lowered himself down the hole on a long silken thread. Anansi the spider swung through the starry sky, past the moon, past leaves and through branches. He dropped into a sunny day, landed on the mossy bank, and turned himself back into a man.

There sat the wrinkled old woman with a pile of empty shells in her lap.

"Mmmm hmmm," she said, "Are you hungry?"

"Yes," said Anansi, brushing the crumbs from his mouth.

"Well, there are lots of sweet potatoes growing in the field," the old woman replied. "The big potatoes are calling '*Eat me!*' and the little potatoes are calling '*Don't eat me!*' Dig up the little potatoes and bring them to me."

20

Anansi took the spade, and went into the field. The huge, juicy potatoes were calling *"Eat me, eat me!"* The tiny shrivelled potatoes were calling *"Don't eat me, don't eat me!"*

"I am not eating those dried-up things!" he complained. So Anansi dug the big potatoes up.

"Now peel the potatoes," said the old woman. "Put the peel in the pot and throw away the insides."

Anansi had never heard anything so ridiculous. But he peeled the potatoes. The peel was covered in grit and mud.

"Ugghh," he shivered, "I can't possibly eat that!" So he put the juicy insides into the pot, and threw away the peel. The pot began to bubble. Anansi served up the potatoes, making sure he had the biggest helping. Then they sat down to eat.

The old woman picked up her spoon, and began eating through her nose, and eating through her ears.

"How disgusting!" cried Anansi. "Have you no manners? You should eat like me."

He picked up his spoon. "Yuck!" he spluttered. "That tastes revolting." He pushed his bowl away – it was the worst thing he had ever eaten.

"Thank you," said the old woman. "I would like to give you something in return."

She showed him the door at the back of the hut. "Go inside, and choose the smallest drum, take it home, play it and shout COVER!" she advised.

Anansi opened the door. He stared at the biggest drum and thought, "If the little drum gives food, what will the big drum give?"

He snatched up the biggest drum and raced back to the hole. The old woman didn't even have time to show him the path out of the underworld.

"He hey!" laughed Anansi. "This drum will give me ten times more food, and probably gold as well."

He turned himself back into spider, spun a web and wove a thread round the drum. Then he began to pull himself, and the drum out of the hole. The drum was heavy and it was a long way up.

A very long way up. Panting and groaning Anansi pulled the drum through branches, past leaves, past the moon, through the starry sky and back into our world.

Then he turned himself into a man, and
carried the drum home.

When he arrived everyone was asleep.
"Good!" he whispered. "I won't have to
share my drum with anyone."

He sat down and, very quietly, he began
to play.

Ta, te, ta te te, ta ta taa.

Faster and faster and faster.

Ta te, ta te te, ta ta TAA!

"COVER!" he cried.

Suddenly Anansi was covered in spots.
Covered in huge red and yellow and green
spots!

"*Ahhhhh!*" he screamed.

He was covered in spots from head to
toe!

"*Help!*" he shouted.

Everyone woke up and rushed outside to see what the matter was. Anansi was rolling on the ground, covered in spots. His children began to laugh. Mrs Anansi shook her head and said, "Oh dear, you must be very ill, Anansi. Very ill indeed. You must go to bed right now and stay there until all the spots have gone. And with spots that colour, you better not eat anything.

So Anansi lay in bed for a whole week. He listened to his daughter playing her drum and shouting "COVER!" and everyone feasting and having a good time. Everyone except Anansi. Because he wasn't allowed a crumb.

After that, Anansi never went near the drum, or down to the Underworld, ever again.

Mmmm hmmm!
Anansi made his fun.
And me, I want none.

(Original story from West Africa)

THE GIRL WHO LOVED FOOD

Once there was a cook called Gretel. She worked for a rich man, and lived in the attic at the top of his house. Gretel had the most beautiful pair of red shoes. Every morning she would put on her shoes, stand in front of the mirror, turn this way and that, click her heels together, and say, "Gretel, you are the cleverest cook in the land!" Then she would set about her day's work, for she was an excellent cook, and loved good food and good wine.

As soon as her Master was out, Gretel would sneak down to the cellar and pour herself a glass of wine. "Here's to you, Gretel!" she would say, raising the glass and gulping down the wine. This made her very hungry. So she would go back to the kitchen and cook herself the best bacon and eggs, taking care to wipe the grease from both corners of her mouth so that her master would be none the wiser.

One day her Master came into the kitchen. "A Very Important Guest is coming for supper tonight," he announced. "I want to impress him. Roast two chickens and make sure they are cooked perfectly. If they are even the tiniest bit burnt, Gretel, you are out."

So Gretel put on her apron and went into the yard. She caught two chickens. She chopped off their heads, and chopped off their tails. She pulled out their insides, and plucked out their feathers. She basted them well, then put them on the spit over the fire, and turned the spit round and round.

Soon the meat began to cook. The juices sizzled on the coals below and the skin began to crisp and crinkle. The chickens smelt delicious. Gretel called to her Master, "Sir, the chickens are nearly cooked."

"Good, good!" said her Master, rubbing his hands. "I will go and fetch the guest." And he put on his hat and coat and went out into the windy night.

Gretel sat by the fire and turned the spit. It was hot and thirsty work. So she sneaked down to the cellar and poured herself a large glass of wine. "Here's to you, Gretel!" she said, gulping it down. This made her very hungry.

She went back to the kitchen and looked at the chickens. "Oh dear!" she said "One of the wings is a tiny bit burnt. My Master will not be pleased." And quick as a flash, she pulled the burnt wing off. Now he would be none the wiser!

She looked at the crispy, brown wing. "It would be a shame to waste it," she thought. so she tasted it, and it was delicious.

"Oh dear!" she said. "Now the chicken has one wing on and one wing off. That will never do. I'd better pull the other wing off and even it up." And off came the second wing, and it would be a shame to waste it, so she ate it.

"Oh dear!" she said. "Now one chicken has wings and one chicken has none. I'd better pull off the other wings then he won't notice the difference." And off came the other two wings, and it would be a shame to waste them, so down they went the same way.

Then Gretel ran to the window and
looked out. There was no sign of her
Master or the Guest. All she could see was
lashing rain.

"Perhaps they are waiting until the rain
stops?" she thought. "It would be a shame
to waste the chickens. Someone should eat
them. And the only someone here...
is me!"

So Gretel pulled one chicken off the spit then sat down at the kitchen table and gobbled it up. She smacked her lips, and looked longingly at the other chicken.

"Oh dear!" she said. "Now you're lonely. You chickens hatched together, scratched in the yard together, were roasted together, and now you're apart. Gretel," she said to herself, "be kind and send that chicken down to its friend."

And that is just what she did. Gretel
pulled the second chicken off the spit, and
soon there was a huge pile of bones on
her plate. She was just wiping the grease
from both corners of her mouth, when she
heard the front door open. It was the
Master.

"The Guest is on his way, Gretel," he called out. "The chickens smell excellent. I am just going to open a bottle of wine, and sharpen the carving knife."

The Master went into the dining room. He opened the wine and picked up the sharpening stone. He began to swipe the blade of the carving knife back and forth across the stone.

SHHHT ... SHHHT ... SHHHT!

Then there was a polite tap at the front door, Gretel smoothed her apron and went to answer the door. There stood a large man.

"I am the Very Important Guest," he said. "I have come to supper."

"Uhh..." said Gretel, thinking very fast. "Can you hear that noise?"

The Guest listened and heard, SHHHT ... SHHHT ... SHHHT, coming from the dining room. "It sounds like someone sharpening the carving knife," said the Guest. "It must be meat we are having for supper." And he patted his Very Important Stomach.

"Yes, it is meat," said Gretel quickly, "and the meat is going to be you!"

"Don't be ridiculous," laughed the Guest.

"But sir, my Master is a very evil man," whispered Gretel urgently. "He invites people to dinner, then ties them to a chair. He cuts off both their ears, roasts them on a spit, and serves the ears up on toast!

Please sir, run away from here as fast as you can."

SHHHT ... SHHHT ... SHHHT! The knife sounded very sharp indeed, and the Guest turned on his heels and ran.

Then Gretel flew into the dining room, raised her hands in the air, and cried, "Oh, Master, your Very Important Guest has just come into the kitchen, taken the chickens, and run off with them!"

"What!" shouted the Master. "But I'm starving. Didn't he even leave one chicken?"

"No sir," said Gretel, "he took them both."

"Greedy fellow," snorted the Master. "I'm going to get one back."

With that the Master ran out of the house, waving the carving knife in the air and calling, "Come back here, you scoundrel! That's my supper you're running away with! Just let me have one, you can keep the other one. Please... just one!"

The poor Guest thought he meant just one ear. He clapped his hands over his ears and ran even faster. The Guest ran and the Master ran, until the Guest came to his own front door. He rushed inside and bolted the door tight. He sighed with relief: he still had both his ears! The Master went home wet and bedraggled, and very hungry.

But as for Gretel, she looked in the mirror, turned this way and that, clicked her red heels together and said, "Gretel, what a clever cook you are."

For she was full, and she was merry, and no one was any the wiser. Except for you!

(Original story from Germany)